Friends Get Together

Metro Early Reading Program

Level B, Stories 1–5

Credits
Illustration: Front cover, Pat Paris
Photography: Front and back covers, Mark Segal/Tony Stone Images

ISBN 1-58120-646-1

2 3 4 5 6 7 8 9 CL 03 02 01 00

Table of Contents

A
Bag
for
Dad

Dad just has that old bag for work.
Would he like a new bag for
his birthday?
Which bag would make a good
work bag, Grandmother?

2

3

4

6

7

I will take this tan bag for my dad.
Can you put a little tag on the box?
Put on the tag To Dad, From Jed.

I will take this red bag for my grandmother.
Can you put a little tag on the box?
Put on the tag <u>To Grandmother, From Nan</u>.

13

15

16

When Will the Sun Come Out?

When will the sun come out, Dad?
I can not have fun in here.
I would like to go out and play.

18

19

We are here for
a picnic.
I have my sun hat.
Marta has a mat
that we can sit on.

How can we have a picnic?
We would get so wet
out there.

22

Then we will have a picnic in here.
I will put down the mat.
We have buns.
We have ham and jam.

25

We do not have sun.
But I know what
can do the job.
You will see.

27

28

34

37

I have an old bicycle.
It is not any good.
I have to have a nice
new one.
Then the two of us
can ride.

39

41

The two of us can work on your bicycle.
We can make it as good as new.

45

47

48

51

Here are the games.
We can bat and race.
We can hit pins down.
We can hop.

52

53

54

I know what I said before.
I know you came to play.
You can hop for our team,
Tasha.
You are good at that.

55

59

61

63

Story 5

Come in, Jed.
Did you see Boo
when you came in?
I do not know if
he got out.

67

Boo is not on my bed.
He likes to nap there
in the sun.
But he is not there.

68

70

71

75

I see Tasha on her bicycle.
And I see Ben.
They can come with us
to get Boo.

76

87

There is a cat here.
He is very tame
and very nice.

He came to play
with my cat.
The two cats play
a game with that bag.
It is a game they
like very much.

93

Skills and Vocabulary

Story 1: A Bag for Dad

First Review

initial consonant:
t

New

phonograms:
-ag, -an

decodable words:
bag, dad, Nan, tag, tan

sight words:
much, old, take, which

story words:
birthday, grandmother

Skills and Vocabulary

Story 2: When Will the Sun Come Out?

New

phonograms:
-am, -ob, -un

decodable words:
bun, fun, ham, jam, job, sun, wet

sight words:
know, when

story words:
picnic, surprise

Story 3: Side by Side

First Review

initial consonant:
hard g

New

phonograms:
-ice, -ide

decodable words:
got, nice, ride, side, wide

sight words:
an, any, as, by, two

story word:
bicycle

Skills and Vocabulary

Story 4: Game Day

First Review

initial consonant:
hard c

New

phonograms:
-ace, -ame

decodable words:
came, game, pin, race, run, same

sight words:
before, said, they

story words:
school, team

Story 5: Did You See Boo?

Review Story

No new phonics elements or sight words.